STAR TREK
THE WRATH OF KHAN
PHOTOSTORY

BY RICHARD J. ANOBILE

BASED ON A SCREENPLAY BY JACK B. SOWARDS
STORY BY HARVE BENNETT
AND JACK B. SOWARDS

PUBLISHED BY POCKET BOOKS NEW YORK

ANAMORPHIC FRAME BLOWUPS BY RYAN HERZ & MARK HENRY.
INTERIOR DESIGN BY HARRY CHESTER ASSOCIATES.

"Captain's log.
Stardate 8130.3.
Starship *Enterprise*
on training mis-
sion to Gamma
Hydra. Section 14,
coordinates
22/87/4.

Approaching Neutral Zone. All systems functioning."

"Captain, I'm getting something on the distress channel. Minimal signal, but something."

"Can you amplify?"
"I'm trying."
"On speakers!"

A shaken voice erupts over the bridge's speaker system. "Imperative! Imperative! This is the *Kobayashi Maru.* We have struck a gravitic mine. *Enterprise,* our position is Gamma Hydra, Section 10. Hull penetrated. Life-support systems failing. Many casualties. Can you assist us, *Enterprise?*"

"Mr. Sulu, plot an intercept course!"

"May I remind the Captain that if a Starship enters the Neutral Zone . . ."

"I'm aware of my responsibilities, Mr. Sulu!"

"Now entering the Neutral Zone. Estimating two minutes to intercept."

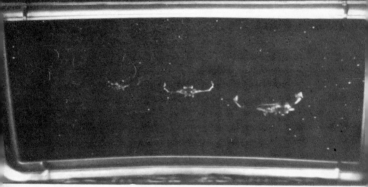

"Captain, I've lost their signal! And sensors indicate three Klingon cruisers, bearing 316 mark 4, closing fast."

"Visual!"

"Battle stations! Activate shields! We're over our heads. Mr. Sulu, get us out of here!"

"I'll try, Captain."

But Saavik's orders are too late. The Klingons fire.

A flustered Saavik shouts, "Evasive action!" But that order, too, comes late.

"Fire all phasers,"
orders Saavik.

Spock quietly answers.
"No power to the
weapons system,
Captain."

Suddenly, another torpedo strikes a deadly blow.

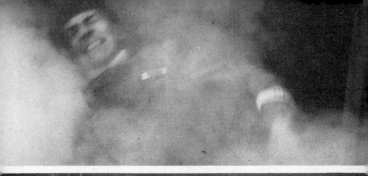

The *Enterprise* is dead in space.

As Saavik sits in a stupor, Admiral Kirk's voice booms over loud-
speakers.
"All right, open her up."

The lights come up, and there is a loud clanging as Kirk enters the bridge.

And Spock comes alive.

Saavik at attention.
"I don't believe this was a fair test of my command capabilities, sir. There was no way to win."

Kirk is terse.
"A no-win situation is a possibility every commander may face. Has that never occurred to you?"

"No, sir. It has not."

"How we deal with death is at least as important as how we deal with life, wouldn't you say, Saavik?"

"As I indicated, Admiral, that thought had not occurred to me."

"Then you have something new to think about. Carry on."

MOMENTS LATER.

"Aren't you dead?"

"Well, Spock, your cadets destroyed the simulator room and you with it."

"The *Kobayashi Maru* scenario frequently wreaks havoc with students and equipment. As I recall, you took the test three times yourself. Your final solution was, shall we say, unique?"

"It had the virtue of never having been tried."

Kirk continues. "By the way, thank you for this book."

"I know your fondness for antiques."

Kirk quotes from the book. " 'It was the best of times, it was the worst of times.' Message, Spock?"

"None of which I am consciously aware . . . except, of course, happy birthday. Surely, the best of times."

LATER THAT NIGHT.

"Romulan Ale! Bones, you know this stuff is illegal!"

"Oh, don't be such a prig! While I pour, open the other gift."

"I'm almost afraid to! What did you bring me, Klingon contraband? What are these?"

"For your eyes. Four hundred years old. You don't find many with the lenses still intact. Happy birthday. Cheers!"

"Amazing! I don't know what to say."

"Say thank you, Jim."

"Thank you."

"Damn it, Jim! What the hell's the matter? Other people have birthdays. Why're we treating yours like a funeral?"

"Bones, I don't want to be lectured."

"Jim, I'm your doctor and your friend. Get back your command. Get it back before you really do grow old and turn into part of this collection."

IN DEEP SPACE
THE U.S.S. *RELIANT*
NEARS CETI ALPHA V.

"Starship log. Stardate 8130.4. This report classified MOST SECRET. Log entry by Commander Pavel Chekov, Duty Officer. Starship U.S.S. *Reliant* on orbital approach with Ceti Alpha VI in connection with project, code name Genesis. We are continuing our search for a lifeless planet which will serve as a suitable test site for the Genesis Experiments. This is the sixteenth planet we have visited; so far, no success."

"Captain Terrell, does it have to be completely lifeless?" asks Chekov. "We've picked up a minor energy flux reading on one scanner."

"Damn!" says Terrell. "Let's get on the horn to Dr. Marcus. Maybe it's something we can transplant."

"You know what she'll say!" sighs Chekov.

SPACE STATION
REGULA I.

"Something you can
transplant?"
asks Carol Marcus.
"I don't know—"

Terrell interrupts.
"It might only be a
particle of preanimate
matter . . ."

"Then again, it might
not. You boys have
to be clear on this.
There can't be so
much as a microbe
or the show's off."

"Why don't you
have a look,"
decides Marcus.
"If it *is* something
that can be
moved . . ."

Terrell is quick to
agree. "You bet,
Doctor. We're on
our way."

MOMENTS LATER.

"Well," says David, "don't have kittens. Genesis is going to work. They'll remember you in one breath with Newton, Einstein, Surak . . ."

"Thanks a lot!" sighs Marcus. "No respect from my offspring."

"Mom, every time we have dealings with Star-fleet I get nervous. We're dealing with something that could be perverted into a dreadful weapon. Remember that overgrown boy scout you used to hang out with? That's exactly the—"

Carol is somewhat annoyed.
"Listen, kiddo, Jim Kirk was many things, but he was never a boy scout!"

THE SURFACE OF CETI ALPHA V.

Terrell is confused.
"Chekov, are you sure these coordinates are right? I can hardly see."

Chekov affirms. "There's nothing. Let's go."

Terrell spots something familiar. "Wait. Those look like cargo carriers."

Terrell and Chekov take a closer look. "Give me a hand with this door."

Both men enter the
carrier.
"What the hell is this?"
asks Terrell. "There's
breathable air in here!"

Then Chekov notices a familiar name on an old seat belt buckle.
Botany Bay. Oh, no!"

"Captain, we've got to get out of
here *now!* Damn! Hurry!"

. . . it's too late.

But by the time they get
outside . . .

LATER.

"Khan!"

"I never forget a face. Mr. Chekov, isn't it?"

Terrell is puzzled. "Chekov, who is this man?"

"A criminal, Captain. A product of late 20th century genetic engineering."

Terrell addresses Khan. "What do you want with us? I demand . . ."

"You are in a position to demand nothing, sir. I, on the other hand, am in a position to grant nothing. What you see is all that remains of the ship's company and crew of the *Botany Bay*, marooned here fifteen years ago by Captain James T. Kirk."

"Do you mean that Chekov never told you how the *Enterprise* picked up the *Botany Bay,* lost in space from the year 1996, myself and the ship's company in cryogenic freeze?"

"I've never met Admiral Kirk. . . ."

"Admiral!
He didn't tell you how *Admiral* Kirk sent seventy of us into exile on this barren sand heap with only the contents of these cargo bays to sustain us?"

Chekov screams.
"You lie! On Ceti Alpha V there was life, a fair chance to—"

Khan explodes.
"*This* is Ceti Alpha V! Ceti Alpha VI exploded six months after we were left here. The shock shifted the orbit of this planet and everything was laid waste. *Admiral* Kirk never bothered to check on our progress. Only my genetically engineered intellect enabled us to survive."

"You didn't expect to find me. You thought this was Ceti Alpha VI. Why are you here?"

Suddenly Khan grabs Chekov and, in a display of superhuman strength, lifts him into the air saying, "Why?"

A startled Chekov is silent.
"No matter," sighs Khan.

"You will soon tell me willingly enough."

"Let me introduce you to Ceti Alpha V's only remaining indigenous life form."

"What do you think? They've killed twenty of my people, including my beloved wife."

Khan plucks two of the Ceti eel's offspring from between its armor.

"Oh, not all at once, and not instantly, to be sure."

"Their young enter through the ears and wrap themselves around the cerebral cortex."

Khan places the young creatures into the helmets of Chekov and Terrell.

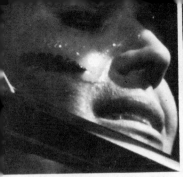

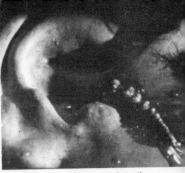

"This has the effect of rendering the victim extremely susceptible to suggestion."

The creatures move into the men's ears.

"Later, as they grow, follow madness, paralysis and death."

After the initial pain, the men calm down.
"That's better! Now, tell my why you are here. And tell me where I may find James Kirk."

AT THAT MOMENT, IN
ANOTHER PART OF THE
GALAXY, A SPACE
SHUTTLE APPROACHES
THE *ENTERPRISE.*

"*Enterprise,* this is Admiral Kirk's party on final approach."

"*Enterprise* welcomes you. Prepare for docking."

MOMENTS LATER.

"Permission to come aboard, Captain?"

"Welcome aboard, Admiral."

"I believe you know my trainee crew," adds Spock. "Certainly they have come to know you."

"Yes, we've been through death and life together," quips Kirk.

"Mr. Scott, you old space dog! You're well?"

"I had me a wee bout, but Dr. McCoy pulled me through."

"Oh? A wee bout of what, Mr. Scott?"

"Shore leave," Bones interjects.

Kirk moves on. "Ah. Well, shall we start with the engine room?"

"I'll see you there, Admiral," says Scott. Then adds, "I believe you'll find all in order."

"That would be a pleasant surprise, Mr. Scott."

As Kirk leaves for the engine room, Saavik seems puzzled. "He's not what I expected, sir."

"What surprises you, Lieutenant?"

"He's very human."

"Saavik, nobody's perfect!"

LATER—ENGINE ROOM.

"Very well, Mr. Scott. Are your engines capable of handling a minor training cruise?"

"Give the word, Admiral."

"Mr. Scott, the word is given."

"Aye, sir."

As a turbo lift begins to take Kirk to the bridge, Bones quickly asks, "What about the rest of the inspection, Admiral?"

Anxious to get under way, Kirk whispers, "Later!"

"This is Starfleet Operations. *Enterprise* is cleared for departure."

As Kirk gazes about his old command post, Spock's voice ripples through the bridge.
"Mr. Saavik, you may clear all moorings."

"All moorings are clear, Captain."

"Lieutenant, how many times have you piloted a Starship out of spacedock?"

"Never, sir."

As Kirk and Bones look on in disbelief, Spock issues his next command.
"Take her out, Mr. Saavik."
"Aye, sir."

Aware of the anxiety he has caused—and enjoying it—Spock adds, "For everything there is a first time, Lieutenant."

Saavik proceeds.
"Aft thrusters, Mr. Sulu."

Sulu responds.
"Aft thrusters, sir."

And the *Enterprise* begins to leave its dock.

"Course heading, Captain?"

"Mr. Sulu, you may indulge yourself."
"Aye, sir!"

SPACE STATION
REGULA I

"Come in please. This is *Reliant* calling *Regula I*. Repeat.
This is *U.S.S. Reliant . . .*"

"Commander, we are receiving."

"Dr. Marcus, we're en route to you and should be there in three days."

"En route? We weren't expecting you for another three months!
Has something happened?"

"We have received new orders.
Upon our arrival all materials of
Project Genesis will be transferred
to this ship for immediate testing
at Ceti Alpha VI."

"But Genesis is a civilian project
under my control!"

"I have my orders."

David interrupts.
"Pin him down, mother! Who gave
the orders?"

"The orders come from Admiral James T. Kirk. Doctor, Admiral Kirk's orders are confirmed. Please prepare to deliver Genesis to us. *Reliant* out."

Khan gloats. "Well done, Commander."

"You realize that they will attempt to contact Admiral Kirk and confirm that order," says Chekov.

Khan smiles knowingly.

LATER.

"Jim, can you read me?"

"Carol, what's wrong?"

"Why are you taking Genesis away from us?"

The transmission begins to fade. "Taking Genesis! Who is taking Genesis?"

"I can see you but can't hear! Did you order . . ."

"What order? Who's taking Genesis?"

"Please help us, Jim! I won't let them have . . ."

"Carol! Uhura! What's happening?"

"Transmission jammed at the source, Admiral."

"Damn! Alert Starfleet Headquarters. I want to talk with Starfleet Command."

A WHILE LATER.

Spock is meditating as Kirk
enters quietly and speaks.

"We've got a problem."

"Something may be wrong
at *Regula I.* We've been
ordered to investigate. I
told Starfleet all we had
was a shipload of children,
but we're the only ship in
the quadrant. Spock, how
good are they? How will
they respond under real
pressure?"

"Like all living beings,
Admiral, each according to
his gifts. The ship is yours."

"That won't be necessary.
Just take me to *Regula I.*"

"You proceed from a false assumption. I am a Vulcan. I have no ego to bruise."

"You are going to remind me that logic alone dictates your actions."

"I was going to remind you of nothing, least of all that which you know well."

"Your mistake, if I may be so bold, was promotion. Commanding a Starship is your first best destiny. Anything else is a waste of material."

"I would not presume to debate you."

"That is wise. In any case, were I to invoke logic, logic clearly dictates that the needs of the many outweigh the needs of the few."

"Or the one." Adds Kirk.

Spock continues.
"You are my superior officer. You are also my friend. I have been and always shall be yours."

THE BRIDGE—
MOMENTS LATER.

"An emergency situation has arisen. By order of Starfleet Command, as of now, 1800 hours, I am assuming command of this vessel."

"Duty Officer, so note in the ship's log. Plot a new course for Space Laboratory *Regula I.*"

"Engage warp engines."

"Prepare for
warp speed."

With a bit of a gleam in his eye, Kirk gives Sulu the order.
"Take her to warp speed five!"

As Kirk leaves the bridge for a moment, Sulu mutters to himself.
"So much for the training cruise."

And the *Enterprise* goes to warp speed.

Uhura's voice beams a message through space. *"Regula I,* this is *Enterprise.* This is *Enterprise.* Do you receive? Do you receive?"

"It's no use, sir. No response from *Regula I."*

"But no longer jammed?"

"No, sir. No, nothing."

"Admiral, there are two possibilities. They are unwilling to respond; they are unable to respond."

"How far?"

"Twelve hours and forty-three minutes, present speed."

"Give up Genesis, she said! Give it up to whom?"

"It might help my analysis if I knew what Genesis was, beyond the biblical sense of the word."

"Uhura, ask Dr. McCoy to join us in my quarters. And Mr. Saavik, you have the com."

"Computer. Request access to Project Genesis Summary."

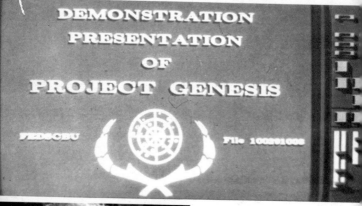

"I'm Dr. Carol Marcus, and I am director of the Project Genesis team at *Regula I.* What exactly is Genesis? Put simply, Genesis is life from lifelessness."

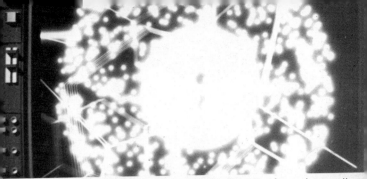

"It is a procedure whereby the molecular structure of any given matter can be restructured into life-generating matter."

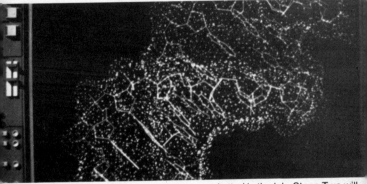

"Stage One of our experiments was conducted in the lab. Stage Two will be attempted in a lifeless underground. Stage Three will involve the process on a planetary scale. Please watch the following simulation of Stage Three."

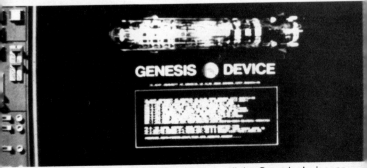

GENESIS ● DEVICE

"It is our intention to introduce what we call the Genesis device, or torpedo, into the targeted area . . ."

". . . of a lifeless
space body, a
moon or other
inert form. The
device is
fired . . ."

". . . unleashing,
almost
instantaneously,
what we call the
Genesis effect.

Particulate matter
is reorganized
and electrified with
life-introduced
results."

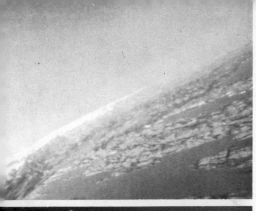

"Instead of a dead moon, a living, breathing planet capable of sustaining life."

"The re-formed object you see represents the merest fraction of the Genesis potential."

"When we consider the problems of population and food supply, the usefulness of this process begins to become clear."

Spock is impressed.
"It literally is
Genesis."

Kirk is amazed.
"The power of
creation."

Bones is concerned.
"But dear Lord, are we intelligent enough to . . . Suppose this thing was
used where life already exists?"

Spock answers matter-of-factly.
"It would destroy such life in favor of its new matrix."

Bones fumes.
"Its new . . . ! Have you any idea what you're saying?"

"I was not attempting to
evaluate its moral implica-
tions, Doctor. As a matter
of cosmic history, it has
always been easier to
destroy than to create."

"Not anymore! Now you can do both at the same time! According to myth, the earth was created in six days. Watch out, here comes Genesis! We'll do it for you in six minutes!"

Spock maintains his calm.
"Really, Dr. McCoy. You must learn to govern your passions. They will be your undoing."

Bones is now shouting.
"We're talking about universal Armageddon . . . you inhuman, greenblooded . . ."

Saavik's voice interrupts Bones's tirade.
"Admiral, sensors indicate a vessel in our area, closing fast."

"What do you make of her?"

"It's one of ours, Admiral. It's *Reliant.*"

"*Reliant*? Chekov's on *Reliant.*"

"*Reliant* in our section this quadrant, sir, and slowing."

Saavik is direct. "Sir, may I quote General Order 12. On the approach of any vessel, when communications have not been . . ."

Spock interrupts. "Lieutenant, the Admiral is aware of the regulations!"

A chastened Saavik says, "Aye, sir."

Meanwhile, the *Reliant* moves closer.

"The *Enterprise* is still running with shields down," says Khan's helmsman.

"Of course," gleams Khan. "We're one big happy fleet. Ah, Kirk my old friend! Do you know the Klingon proverb that tells us revenge is a dish that is best served cold? It is very cold in space."

The two ships now approach each other.

"This is damn peculiar. Yellow alert!"

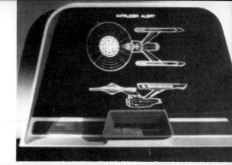

"Energize defense field."

"Raise shields. Lock on target—the engine room—and prepare to fire."

"Locking phasers on target."

"Fire!"

"Mr. Sulu, the shields!"   "I'm trying, sir! I can't get power!"

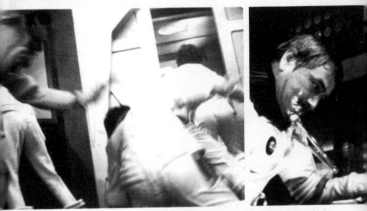

The cadets in the engine room are panicked and running from their posts. Scotty reports to Kirk. "Main energizers out."

"They knew just where to hit us, Admiral."

"Who? And why?"

"One thing is certain. We cannot escape on auxiliary power."

As Kirk and Spock discuss their dilemma, Khan strikes again.

This time at the bridge.

"Scotty, what's left?"

"Just the batteries. I can have auxiliary power in a few minutes."

"We don't have minutes! Can you give me phaser power?"

"A few shots, sir."

"Not enough against their shields."

"Admiral, Commander, *Reliant* is signaling. He wishes to discuss terms of our surrender."

"Put it on screen. Do it while we still have time."

"On screen, sir."

"Khan!"

"You still remember, Admiral! I cannot help but be touched. Of course, *I* remember *you*."

"What is the meaning of this attack? Where is the crew of the *Reliant?*"

"Surely I have made my meaning plain. I mean to avenge myself upon you, Admiral. I've deprived your ship of power, and when I swing around I mean to deprive you of your life."

"But I wanted you to know first who it was who had beaten you."

"Khan, if it's me you want,
I'll have myself beamed
aboard. Spare my crew."

"I make you a counterproposal. I will agree to your terms if, in addition to
yourself, you turn over to me all data and material regarding the project
called Genesis."

"Genesis? What's that?"

"Don't insult my intelli-
gence!"

"Give me some time to
recall the data on our computers. . . ."

"I give you sixty seconds,
Admiral."

Kirk whispers.
"At least we know he hasn't got it. Just keep nodding as though I'm giving orders. Saavik, punch up the data charts on *Reliant's* command console."

"The prefix code?" asks Spock.

"It's all we've got."

"Admiral!" shouts Khan.

"We're finding it. Please, you've got to give us time. The bridge is smashed, computers inoperative . . ."

"Time is a luxury you do not have, Admiral. Forty-five seconds!"

"I don't understand," says Saavik.

Kirk is brief. "You've got to learn *why* things work on a Starship."

Spock calmly explains.
"*Reliant's* prefix code is 16309. Each ship has its own prefix combination code, Mr. Saavik."

Kirk continues.
"To prevent an enemy from doing just what we're attempting: using our console to tap in a message to order that *Reliant's* damn shields be lowered."

"Let's hope he hasn't changed the combination. He's quite intelligent," adds Spock.

"Fifteen seconds, Admiral."

"Khan, how do I know you'll keep your word?"

"I've given you no word to keep, Admiral. In my judgment, you simply have no alternative."

"I see your point. Stand by to receive our transmission."

Kirk whispers to Sulu. "Lock phasers on target and await my command."

"Time's up, Admiral."   "Here it comes. Now, Captain Spock."

"Sir, our shields are dropping!"

"Raise them!"

"I can't!"

"Where's the override?"

"Fire!"

"Fire! Fire! Why can't you?"

"We can't fire, sir. They've damaged the photon controls and the warp drive. We must withdraw!"

"No! No!"
"Sir, we must!"

"We must repair the damage. *Enterprise* will wait. She's not going anywhere!"

Reluctantly, the *Reliant* withdraws—for the time being.

"Sir, you did it!"

"I did nothing except get caught with my britches down! I must be senile!
Mr. Saavik, you just keep right on quoting regulations!"

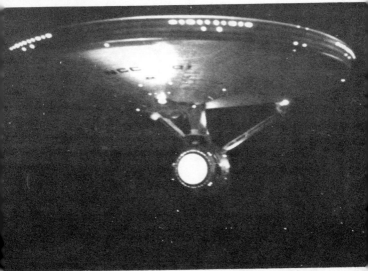

With impulse power restored, the *Enterprise* moves toward Space Station *Regula I.*

"Space Station *Regula I,* this is *Enterprise.* Come in please."

"Hello!" shouts Kirk. "Anybody here?"

Saavik responds.
"Indeterminate life signs."

"Phasers on stun. Move out."

"Jim!"

A stunned Kirk helps Bones cut down the bodies of Khan's massacre.

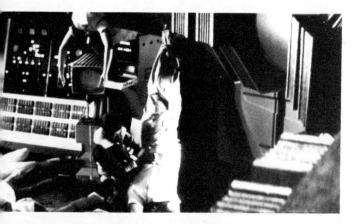

"Rigor hasn't set in. This didn't happen all that long ago, Jim."

Kirk sighs in despair. "Carol," he mutters. But his thoughts are interrupted by Saavik's voice.

"Admiral, over here!"

Saavik's tricorder hums furiously, indicating life.

Kirk, in fearful anticipation, opens the locker. Chekov and Terrell come into view.

"Oh, sir. It was Khan! We found him on Ceti Alpha V. No life signs, but he was there. Captured us and put creatures in our bodies to control our minds. Made us say . . . lies. Do things. But we beat him. He thought he controlled us, but he didn't."

Kirk questions Terrell.

"Captain, where is Dr. Marcus? Where are the Genesis materials?"

"Khan couldn't find them. Even the data banks were empty. He tortured those people. None of them would tell him anything. Then he had to get back to *Reliant* in time to blow you to bits."

"Where is the crew of *Reliant?*"

"Marooned on Ceti Alpha V. He's completely mad, Admiral. He blames you for the death of his wife."

"I know what he blames me for!"

"The escape pods are all in place," notes Kirk. "Where's the transporter room?"

LATER.

"Chekov, did he make it down here?"

"No. He spent most of his time trying to wring the information out of people."

"Somebody left the unit on."

Saavik studies the console.
"This is not logical. These coordinates are well within Regula, a planetoid we know to be lifeless and airless."

Then Kirk realizes what's happened.
"Stage Two was completed. It was underground!"

Saavik is confused.
"Stage Two of what?"

Instead of answering Saavik, Kirk calls the *Enterprise.*
"Damage report, Spock?"

"Admiral, if we go by the book, like Lt. Saavik, hours could seem like days."

"I read you, Captain. Let's have it."

Spock continues.
"The situation is grave, Admiral. We won't have main power for six days at least. Auxiliary power has temporarily failed, but maybe we can restore that in two days. By the book, Admiral."

"Meaning you can't even beam us back."

"Not at present."

"Captain Spock, if you don't hear from us in one hour, your orders are to restore what power you can, take the *Enterprise* to the nearest Star Base, and alert Starfleet Command when you are out of jamming range. Kirk out."

"If it's all the same, Admiral, we'd like to share the risk," says Terrell.

"Very well. Let's go."

"Go?" questions Bones. "Where are we going?"

"Where they went," answers Kirk.

Bones is incredulous.
"But what if they went . . . nowhere?"

Kirk is ironic.
"Then this will be your big chance to get away from it all!"

MOMENTS LATER—THE PLANETOID REGULA.

"Genesis, I presume."

Suddenly a noise startles Kirk.

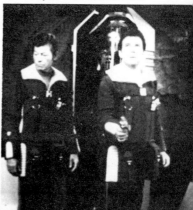

Then . . .

"Where's Dr. Marcus?" screams Kirk.   "Jim!"
"I'm Dr. Marcus!"

"Is that David?"

"Mother, he killed everybody we left behind!"

"Well, of course he didn't! David, you're just making this harder."

Terrell interrupts.
"I'm afraid it's even harder than you think, Doctor. Please don't move."

"Chekov!"

Chekov is torn.
"I'm sorry, Admiral."

Terrell speaks to Khan via his wrist recorder.
"Your excellency, have you been listening?"

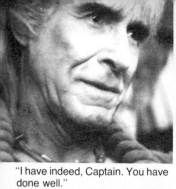

"I have indeed, Captain. You have done well."

"You now have the coordinates to beam up Genesis."

First things first, Captain. Kill Admiral Kirk."

"Excellency, it is difficult. I try to obey, but . . ."

"Kill him!"

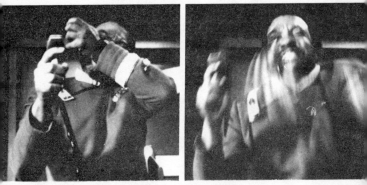

Suddenly Terrell flings off the wrist recorder.

And blows himself into oblivion.

Then Chekov writhes in pain and falls.

"Jim, for God's sake!"

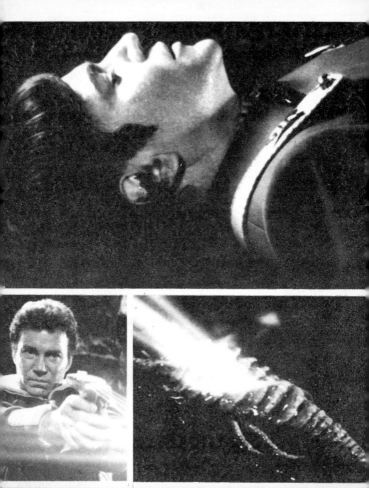

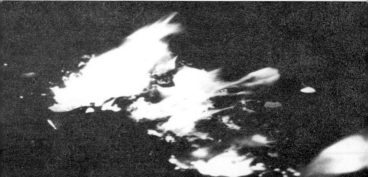

"Khan, you bloodsucker! You'll have to do your own dirty work now. Do you hear me? You've managed to kill just about everyone else, but like a poor marksman you keep missing the target!"

"Perhaps, my old friend, I no longer need to try."

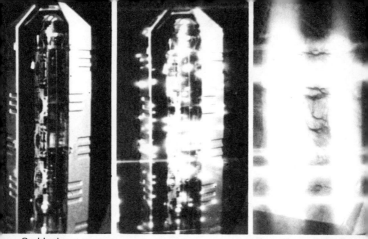

Suddenly . . .

"Let go! He can't . . ."

"Khan, you have Genesis,
but you don't have me! You
were going to kill me, Khan.
Now you'll have to come
down here to do it!"

"I've done far worse than kill you, Admiral. I've hurt you. And I wish to go on hurting you. I shall leave you as you left me, as you left her, marooned for eternity in the center of a dead planet— buried alive."

"Khan, Khan!"

LATER.

Saavik tries the communicator.
"This is Lt. Saavik, calling *Enterprise*. Can you read us?"

"Jim, Chekov's coming around!"

Saavik despairs.
"No use, Admiral, they're still jamming all channels."

"It wouldn't make any difference. If *Enterprise* obeyed orders, she's long since gone. And if she couldn't obey, she's finished."

"Is there anything to eat? I don't know about anyone else, but I'm starved."

Bones is startled. "How can you think of food at a time like this?"

Kirk is logical. "Our first order of business is survival."

"There's food in the Genesis cave," answers Carol. "Enough to last a lifetime—should that be necessary."

Bones is confused.

"We thought this was Genesis!"

"This? It took the Starfleet engineers ten months to tunnel out all this. What we did in here we did in a day. David, why don't you show Dr. McCoy and the lieutenant our idea of food?"

"This is just to give us something to do, isn't it?" shrugs David. "Come on."

Before she goes with David, Saavik gives a somewhat confused look to Kirk, who tells her, "As your teacher, Mr. Spock, is fond of saying, 'I like to think there always are possibilities.' "

Kirk is thoughtful for a moment, then: "I did what you wanted. I stayed away. Why didn't you tell me?"

"How can you ask me that? Were we together? Were we going to be? You had your world and I had mine. I wanted him in mine, not chasing through the universe with his father."

"Actually, he's a lot like you in many ways. Please, tell me what you're feeling."

"There's a man I haven't seen in fifteen years trying to kill me. You show me a son who'd almost be happy to help him. My son. My life that could have been and wasn't. I'm feeling old, worn out."

"Come, let me show you something that will make you feel young—young as when the world was new."

"You did this in a day?"

"The matrix formed in a day. The life forms grew later at a wildly accelerated rate."

Bones shouts to Kirk and Marcus.
"This is incredible!"

"Can I cook
or can't I?"

MEANWHILE,
THE *RELIANT*
SEEKS OUT
THE *ENTERPRISE.*

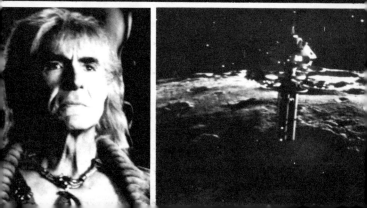

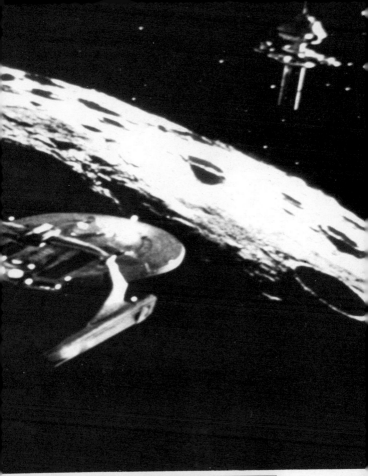

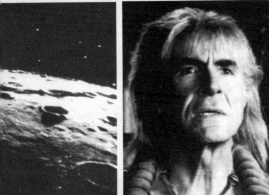

"Where is
she? Where
is she?"

"Admiral, may I ask you a question?"
"What's on your mind, Lieutenant?"
"The *Kobayashi Maru,* sir."

"Are you asking me if we are
playing out that scenario now,
Lieutenant?"

"On the test, sir, will you tell me
what you did? I'd really like to
know."

"Lieutenant, you are looking at the
only Starfleet cadet who ever beat
the no-win scenario."

"How?"
"I reprogrammed the simulation
so it was possible to rescue the
ship."
"What!"

"He cheated!"

"Then," remarks Saavik, "you never faced that situation, faced death . . ."

"I don't believe in a no-win scenario," answers Kirk as he begins to speak into his communicator.
"Spock, this is Kirk. It's two hours. Are you about ready?"

Spock responds.
"Right on schedule, Admiral. Just give us your coordinates and we'll beam you aboard."

"Right!"

Saavik, I don't like to lose."

A SHORT TIME LATER.

Saavik is babbling.
"But the damage report . . .
we were immobilized!"

Kirk smiles.
"Come, come, Lieutenant.
You of all people go by
the book."

"Hello, Spock. You
remember Dr. Marcus."
As Spock and Marcus
greet each other, Saavik
mumbles, "By the book?"

Kirk answers Saavik.
"Regulation 46-A:
'If transmissions are
being monitored
during battle . . ."

Saavik completes the
regulation.
". . . no uncoded messages
on an open channel.' Spock,
you lied," says Saavik.

"I exaggerated," replies Spock.

And Kirk hastily adds, "Hours instead
of days, Saavik. Now we have
minutes instead of hours."

MOMENTS LATER.

An overjoyed Sulu shouts, "Admiral on the bridge!"

"Battle stations!" orders Kirk.

"Tactical."

Spock assesses the situation.
"*Reliant* can outrun us and outgun us. But there is the Mutara nebula at 153 mark four."

Kirk calls the engine room.
"Scotty, can we make it inside?"

"The energizer's bypassed like a Christmas tree, so don't give me too many bumps."

"No promises, Mr. Scott. On your way."

"Trouble with the nebula, sir, is all that static discharge clouds or tactical display," Saavik cautions. "Visuals won't function and shields will be useless."

"Sauce for the goose," comments Spock. Seeing that the comment puzzles Saavik, he adds, "The odds will be even."

AS THE
ENTERPRISE
MOVES TOWARD
THE NEBULA, ITS
CREW PREPARES
FOR BATTLE.

"There she is! Not so wounded as we were led to believe. So much the better!"

"Full impulse power!"

The *Reliant* sprints after *Enterprise*.

"Estimating nebula penetration in two minutes. *Reliant* is closing."

"One minute to nebula perimeter."

"Why are we slowing?"

"We daren't follow them into the nebula, sir; our shields will be useless."

"Admiral, they're reducing speed."

"Uhura, patch me in."

"Aye, sir."

Khan's eyes bulge as Kirk's voice is heard on *Reliant's* bridge. "We tried it once your way, Khan. Are you game for a rematch?"

"Khan! I'm laughing at the 'superior' intellect!"

"Full impulse power!" screams Khan.

Joachim tries to reason with him.
"No, sir! You have Genesis. . . ."

Blind with fury, Khan ignores the advice.
"Full power, damn you!"

As the *Reliant* picks up speed, Kirk remarks, "I'll say this for Khan, he's consistent."

"And we're now entering the Mutara nebula," announces Spock as the *Enterprise* is jolted by electrical charges.

And the *Reliant* follows.

"Tactical!"

"Inoperative."

"Raise the shields!"

"As I feared, sir, not functional. I'm reducing speed."

"Phaser lock inoperative, Admiral."
"Best guess, Mr. Sulu. Fire when ready."

Sulu fires.

As *Reliant* rolls from Sulu's near miss, Khan shrieks, "Aft torpedoes, fire!"

But Khan is no more successful than Sulu.

As both ships maneuver blind, they head into a collision course.

Realizing what is
happening, Kirk shouts,
"Evasive starboard!"
But it is too late.

Reliant fires a series of phaser shots . . .

. . . hitting the *Enterprise*.

"Phaser bank
one, fire!"

Reliant's bridge is hit . . .

. . . and seriously damaged.

"Yours . . . is . . . the superior," gasps Joachim as he dies in Khan's arms.

"I shall avenge you," Khan promises.

MEANWHILE.

With the *Enterprise's* mains off line and radiation leakage preventing their repair, Kirk receives some welcome assistance.
"Could you use another hand, Admiral?"
"Man the weapons console, Mr. Chekov."

"Sporadic energy readings, port side aft. Could be an impulse turn."

"He won't break off now. If he followed me this far he'll be back. But from where?"

"He's intelligent, but not experienced. His pattern indicates two-dimensional thinking."

"Sulu, all stop."

"All stop, sir."

"Z minus thousand meters. Stand by photo torpedoes."

Reliant emerges from the dark mass into a clear, almost tranquil, place.

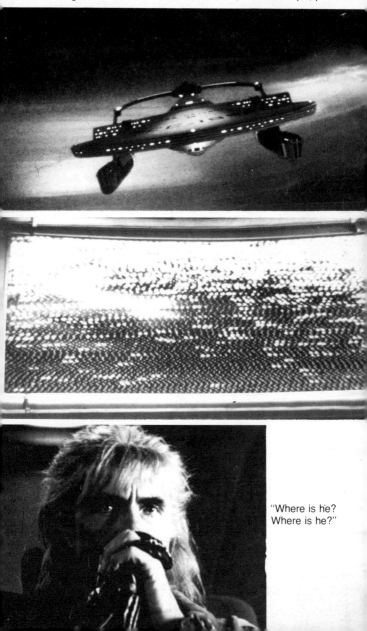

"Where is he?
Where is he?"

The *Enterprise* rises from the depths of space behind *Reliant*.

"Torpedoes ready, sir."   "Look sharp."

Finally, the *Enterprise* screen shows a glimmer of *Reliant*.

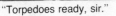

"Fire!"

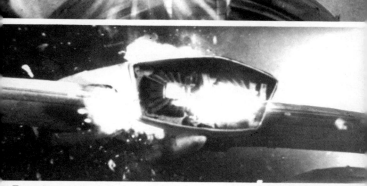

Torpedo one hits *Reliant*, destroying its weapons pod.

Kirk fires two more times. The first shot causes general damage.

The second, close behind, blasts *Reliant's* port engine off into space.

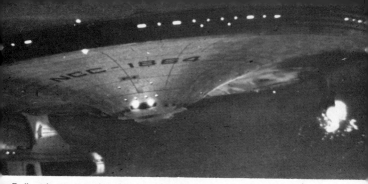

Reliant is a scarred and battered hulk, dead in space.

"Uhura, send to Commander, *Reliant*: Prepare to be boarded."

"Commander, *Reliant*, this is *Enterprise* . . ."

Uhura's voice reverberates through Khan's fire-scarred body.
". . . Surrender and prepare to be boarded."

"Repeat. You are ordered to surrender your vessel. Respond."

Propping himself against the Genesis console, Khan finally answers. "No . . . Kirk. The game's not over."

Then Khan uses the last of his life strength to arm the Genesis torpedo.

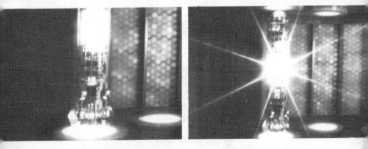

"To the last will I grapple with thee!".

"Admiral! Scanning an energy source on *Reliant*. It's a pattern I've never seen."

"It's the Genesis Wave!" shouts David. "He's on a build-up to detonation!"

"How soon?" asks Kirk.

"We encoded four minutes."

"We'll beam aboard and stop it," Kirk decides.

"You can't!" yells David.

Kirk is frantic.

"Scotty, I need warp speed in three minutes or we're all dead!"

But there is no response from the engine room.

As Spock leaps from his place and leaves the bridge, Kirk shouts, "Saavik, get us out, best speed!"

Enterprise backs away from *Reliant*. Her speed is painfully slow.

Spock rushes to the engine room.

Reliant maintains its deadly course.

Sizing up the situation, Spock starts for the radiation room.

Bones intercepts him.

"Are you out of your Vulcan mind? No human can tolerate the radiation loose in there!"

"But, as you are so fond of observing, Doctor, I'm not human."

"You're not going in there!"

"Perhaps you're right. What is Mr. Scott's condition?"

"Well, I . . .

"Ahhhh . . ."

"Sorry, Doctor, I have no time to discuss this logically."

"Remember."

"Spock! Get out of there!"

"Time from my mark."

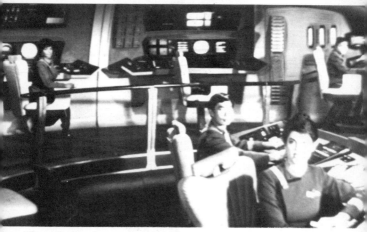

"Two minutes, ten seconds."

"Engine room! What's happening?"

"Spock! Get out, man! Oh, dear God!"

"No, Spock. Don't!"

The *Enterprise* is still within the nebula, and within range of *Reliant*.

"Time!"

"Three minutes, thirty seconds."

"Distance from *Reliant?*"

"Four thousand kilometers."

"We're not going to make it, are we?"

"No!"

"You can't get away!"

"From hell's heart I stab at thee. For hate's sake I spit my last breath at thee!"

"Sir! The mains are back on line!"

"Bless you, Scotty.
Go, Sulu!"

Enterprise goes to warp speed.

And *Reliant* blows.

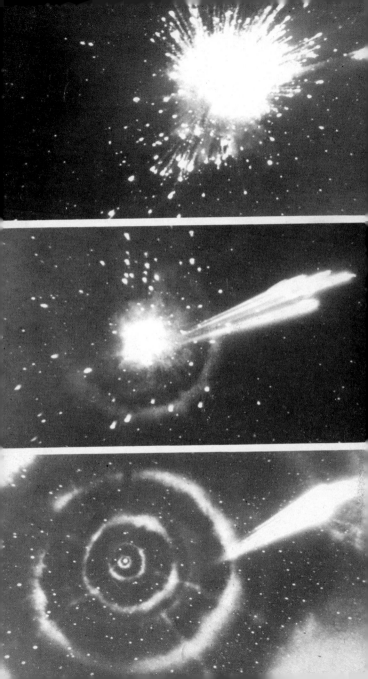

"My God, Carol! Look at it!"

"Engine room. Well done. Scotty?"

Bones's voice answers instead.
"Jim, you better get down here. *Hurry!*"

"Bones?"   "Saavik, take the com."

Krik leaves the bridge. The rest of the crew stare at the new world evolving.

"No, Jim!"

"He'll die!"

"He's dead already!"

"It's too late, Jim!"

Kirk calls to Spock. But Spock does not hear him.

Then Kirk pulls his mind together enough to yell through the speaker system. "Spock!"

Spock struggles to speak.
"Ship . . . out of danger?"

"Yes."

"Don't grieve, Admiral. It's logical. 'The needs of the many out-weigh . . .' "

Spock nods as Kirk completes the quote.
" '. . . the needs of the few . . .' "

" '. . . or the one,' " adds Spock.

"I never took the *Kobayashi Maru* test until now. What do you think of my solution?"

"Spock!"

"I have been . . . and always shall be your friend."

"Live long. And . . . prosper."

"Nooo!"

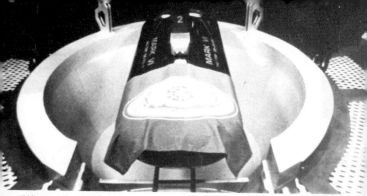

"We are assembled here today to pay final respects to our honored dead."

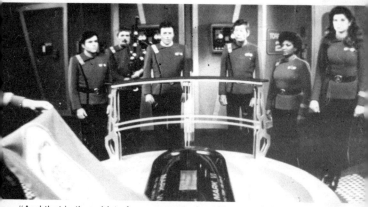

"And that in the midst of our sorrow it should be noted, this death takes place in the shadow of new life, the sunrise of a new world . . ."

". . . A world that our beloved comrade gave his own life to protect and nourish. He did not feel that sacrifice a vain or empty one. And we will not debate his profound wisdom at these proceedings.

"Of my friend, I can only say this: that of all the souls I have encountered in my travels, his was the most . . . human."

"Honors, hup!"

As Scotty begins to pipe "Amazing Grace," the projectile containing Spock's body moves into the launching chamber for Spock's final voyage into space.

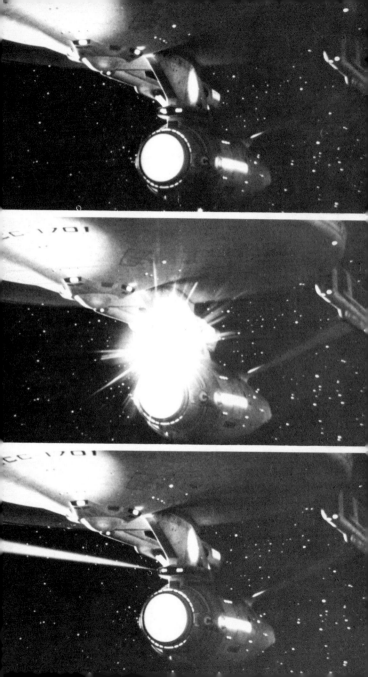

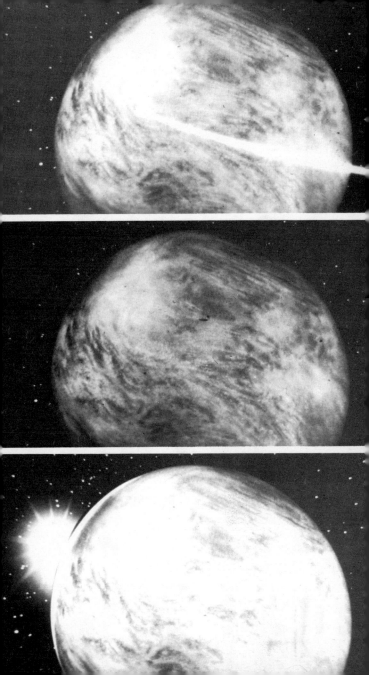

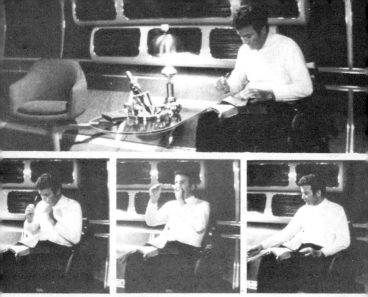

A soft bell breaks Kirk's solitude. "Yes, come in."

"I don't mean to intrude."
"Uh, no. I should be on the bridge."

"Can I talk with you for a minute?"

"I poured a drink. Would you like it?"

"Lieutenant Saavik was right. You never have faced death."

"Not like this, no. I haven't faced death, I cheated death. I tricked my way out of death and patted myself on the back for my ingenuity. I know nothing. It was just words."

"But good words. That's where ideas begin. Maybe you should listen to them. I was wrong about you. And I'm sorry."

"Is that what you came here to say?"

"Mainly."

"And also that I'm proud, very proud, to be your son."

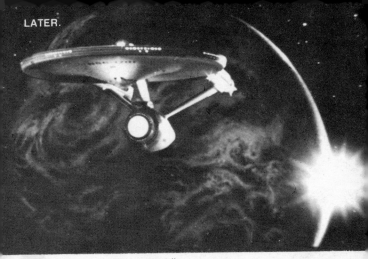

"Captain's log. Stardate 8141.6."

"Starship *Enterprise* departed for Ceti Alpha V to pick up the crew of the U.S.S. *Reliant.* All is well."

"And yet, I can't help wondering about the friend I leave behind."

" 'There are always possibilities,' Spock said. And if Genesis is, indeed, life from death, I must return to this place again."

"He's really not dead as long as we . . . remember him."

"It is a far, far better thing I do than I have ever done before."

"A far better resting place I go to than I have ever known. . . ."

"Is that a poem?" asks Carol.

Kirk thinks a moment.

"Something Spock was trying to tell me . . . on my birthday."

"You okay, Jim? How do you feel?"

"Young! I feel young."

"Space, the final frontier.
These are the voyages of
the Starship *Enterprise*.
Her ongoing mission:
to explore strange new
worlds, to seek out new
life and new civilizations,
to boldly go where no
man has gone before."